WALT DISNEY PICTURES PRESENTS "HERCULES"
MUSIC BY ALAN MENKEN LYRICS BY DAVID ZIPPEL ORIGINAL SCORE BY ALAN MENKEN
SCREENPLAY BY RON CLEMENTS & JOHN MUSKER, BOB SHAW & DON McENERY AND IRENE MECCHI
PRODUCED BY ALICE DEWEY AND JOHN MUSKER & RON CLEMENTS
DIRECTED BY JOHN MUSKER & RON CLEMENTS
DISTRIBUTED BY BUENA VISTA PICTURES DISTRIBUTION, INC. © DISNEY ENTERPRISES, INC.

DISNEP'S
HERCULES

GROLIER
BOOK CLUB EDITION

Listen up, folks, we have a tale to tell.
It's about Hercules, a great hero. Well...

Our story starts long before Hercules was born.
Monsters called Titans made the Earth a terrible place
to live, until Zeus, ruler of the gods, locked them up. He
gave each god a job to bring order to Earth. Now let's
flash forward in time...

...to a party on Mount Olympus. All the gods and goddesses were celebrating the birth of Zeus and Hera's baby boy, Hercules. Zeus made a special gift for his son by shaping clouds into a little winged horse.

"His name is Pegasus," Zeus said, "and he's all yours, Son."

Then the god Hades arrived and threw a dark cloud over the party. Hades ruled the Underworld, and he had never forgiven Zeus for giving him that job. Hades didn't care much for Baby Hercules, either. The kid was too strong!

Hades didn't stay at the party for long. He had a date with the Fates. The three old women could tell him whether his plan to take over Olympus would succeed. They had some news for Hades:

In eighteen years, precisely,
The planets will align ever so nicely.
You and the Titans will cause Zeus to fall.
Then you, Hades, will rule all.
But before Hades could get excited, the Fates added,
A word of caution to this tale:
If Hercules fights, you will fail.

Did that stop Hades? Of course not. He just gave his henchmen, Pain and Panic, a potion that could change a baby god to a baby mortal.

Once little Herc drank every last drop, Pain and Panic could get rid of him for good. Then Hades could defeat Zeus and rule the world.

Well, Pain and Panic stole Baby Hercules and got
him to drink most of the potion. But a mortal couple,
Alcmene and Amphitryon, scared them off before
Hercules could finish the last drops.

So Pain and Panic turned into snakes. But even
though Baby Hercules was human, he still had his
great strength. As they limped away, Pain and Panic
decided not to tell Hades that Hercules was still alive.

The kind mortal couple adopted Baby
Hercules. Zeus and Hera sadly watched their
son grow up on Earth. Since their boy was
mortal, he couldn't be with them on Olympus.
Because Hercules couldn't control his strength,
trouble followed him everywhere. One day he even
knocked down the whole marketplace.

"This is the last straw, Amphitryon!" people shouted.
"Keep him away from here!"

That very night, Amphitryon and Alcmene showed Hercules the medallion that he had been wearing when they found him. Hercules decided that he needed to find out where he belonged.

It was a sad day for his mortal parents. But they kissed their son, and he set off.

 Hercules' first stop was at a temple of Zeus. This was the moment his father had been waiting for. The huge statue of Zeus came to life and smiled at his startled son. "Didn't know you had a famous father, did you?" he chuckled.

That was good news to Herc. At last he knew where he belonged—on Mount Olympus with his dad.

But Zeus had bad news, too. "Only gods can live on Mount Olympus. But if you prove yourself a true hero on Earth, you will be a god again. Find Philoctetes, the trainer of heroes." Then Zeus whistled for Pegasus, who had grown just as much as Hercules.

Hercules jumped onto Pegasus's back with a shout. "I'll find Philoctetes! I'll be a true hero!"

The path to becoming a true hero was full of obstacles.
Philoctetes was the first one. "I'm retired!" he told Hercules.
But, with one last hope of training a genuine hero—and a
little lightning bolt from Zeus—Phil got to work. In time,
Hercules got stronger...and faster...and better all around.

Finally Phil said, "Time for a road test. We're going
to Thebes."

Hercules didn't even get to Thebes before he had his first
test. A young woman named Megara was trying to get away
from the centaur, Nessus. Hercules knocked the horseshoes
right off that centaur. But that was nothing compared to the
way Meg knocked the sandals off Herc.

"M-my name is Hercules," he stammered.

"I think I'll call you 'Wonder Boy,'" Meg told him.
Then she said good-bye.

What Hercules didn't know was that Meg owed Hades a big debt. So Hades wasn't very happy that she had failed to get Nessus to help him fight Zeus.

"It wasn't my fault," Meg told him. "It was this wonder boy, Hercules."

Just the mention of that name made Hades burn.

"Hercules is still around?" he roared at Pain and Panic. But then he glowed thoughtfully. "Well, at least we still have time to correct this...problem."

Meanwhile, the "problem" and his trainer
had arrived in Thebes.

The Thebans weren't interested in Herc's
hero services. But even though the Thebans
wouldn't give Herc a chance to show off, Meg would.
Under Hades' orders, she rushed into town and told
Hercules about two little boys trapped in a rock slide.

Faster than you could say "Corinthian colossus,"
Herc rescued the boys, who were really Pain and Panic
in disguise.

Suddenly a monster—the Hydra—came hissing out
of the ground. The Hydra had a special talent—it
grew three new heads every time Herc lopped off one!
Herc seemed doomed, but he had one trick left. He
caused another rock slide and crushed the Hydra!

From that day on, Herc was famous. He fought lots of monsters—and he had to fight off adoring fans, too.

Everywhere he looked, people were wearing Hercules clothes, drinking Herculade, and buying Hercules action figures.

So Hercules thought it was time to talk to Zeus about getting back to Mount Olympus. But once again, Zeus had bad news for his son. "I'm afraid being famous isn't the same as being a true hero."

"But what more can I do?" Hercules asked.

"It's something you have to discover for yourself," Zeus said. "Look inside your heart."

Now, if you think Hercules was upset, you should
have seen Hades.

He knew Hercules could ruin his plans. "He's got to
have a weakness!" Hades snarled at Meg. If she
could find it, he told her, she could have her freedom.

So Meg spent the day with Hercules trying to discover his weakness. But all she found was a weakness of her own: She was falling in love with the "wonder boy."

Just then, Phil showed up. "All right! Break it up
here!" Phil yelled. He hustled Herc onto Pegasus's
back. As they flew away, Herc was so lovestruck that
he didn't even notice Phil falling off.

Phil landed right near Meg and Hades. He didn't hear Meg tell Hades she was finished helping him. But he did hear Hades tell Meg, "I own you! If I want Wonder Boy—you deliver!"

"This will break the kid's heart," Phil muttered.

As Phil ran off, Meg told Hades, "You can't beat him! He has no weaknesses!"

And that's when it hit Hades—Meg was Herc's weakness!

Herc wouldn't listen to Phil's warning about Meg and Hades. Finally Phil said, "Okay, that's it. I'm hoppin' on the first barge out of here."

As soon as Phil left, Hades showed up with Meg in chains. "If you give up your strength for the next twenty-four hours," Hades offered, "Meg here will be free and safe from harm. But if something should happen to her, you'll get your strength back right away."

When they shook hands on the deal, Hades drained
the strength right out of Hercules. But Hades didn't stop
there. He told Herc that he was planning a change of
address—to Mount Olympus.

"Oh, yes," Hades added. "Remember Meg's plea to save those precious little kids?" As Pain and Panic took the form of two little boys, Hades cackled at the hurt look on Herc's face. The would-be hero finally realized what Meg had done. Meg tried to explain that she had no choice, but Hercules turned away.

Hades' evil plan had worked: Without his strength, Hercules would never be able to keep Hades from taking over Olympus. So, as the planets aligned, Hades was able to go and release the Titans.

"Destroy Zeus!" they roared. As the other Titans thundered toward Olympus, Hades pulled the Cyclops titan aside and sent him to Thebes to destroy Hercules.

The gods put up a good fight, but the winds of the Tornado Titan swept most of them out of action. Zeus found himself facing the Lava Titan and the Ice Titan—one nasty team! The Lava Titan poured molten rock all over Zeus, and the Ice Titan froze it hard. Zeus was trapped, and Hades made himself at home on Olympus.

Things weren't going much better for Herc. He didn't
have the strength left to beat the Cyclops. Meg knew that
he didn't have any hope left, either.

Hopping on Pegasus, she raced to find Phil.

"You're the only one who can give him hope!" Meg
told him. "If you don't help him now, he'll die!"

That made up Phil's mind. He joined Meg and they
hurried back to Hercules.

Herc was down and nearly out for the count when he heard Phil. "You can do it, kid!" Phil shouted. "You can go the distance!"

Now, coming from Phil, that meant a lot. As Hercules gathered the strength he had left, he was scooped up by the Cyclops. But Herc grabbed a burning stick and shoved it at the Cyclops.

Thebes never heard such a howl! The Cyclops dropped Hercules, stumbled, and fell off a cliff.

Meg saw a pillar falling toward Hercules. She pushed him out of the way, but the pillar fell on her.

Now that Meg had been hurt, the deal with Hades had been broken. Hercules' strength returned instantly.

"Why did you risk your life?" Hercules asked.

"People do funny things when they're in love," Meg told him.

Before he left for Olympus, Hercules turned to Phil and said, "Take care of her."

Hercules got to Mount Olympus just as Hades was settling into his new home. In one fell swoop—all right, maybe three—Hercules freed the gods, freed Zeus, and sent the Titans packing.

Hades got in the last word, though, as he headed back to his dark domain. "Well, at least I've got a friend of yours who's dying to meet me."

Hercules raced back to Thebes. But by the time he got
there, Meg's spirit had already slipped from her body.

Phil sighed. "I'm sorry, kid, but there are some things
you just can't change."

Hercules had other ideas. He knew where Meg's spirit
had gone—and he planned on bringing it back.

Hercules burst into Hades' Underworld. "You like deals," he said. "Take me in Meg's place."

Hades had to think about it—for about a second. "Okay," he said. "She goes, you stay."

Hercules plunged into the swirl of spirits. Right away, he started aging. He was nearly ancient by the time he found Meg's spirit.

Then a funny thing happened...only it wasn't very funny to Hades. Hercules began to glow with the brightness of a god. Hades tried to keep him from leaving with Meg's spirit, but Hercules flung the lord of the Underworld down into a bottomless pit. Hades would never trouble either mortals or gods again.

Hercules reunited Meg's spirit with her body, and soon he and Meg were on their way to Olympus. Herc's proud father and mother were waiting for him.

"Fine work, my boy," Zeus said. "Now you know that a true hero is not measured by the size of his strength, but by the strength of his heart. Welcome home."

But Hercules realized that his true home was with Meg, on Earth. So Zeus did one last thing to keep his son up in the heavens. He created an image of Hercules in the stars that would last forever!